Y0-BEA-729

4 2539 00009 8209

WITHDRAWN

Return to
CHILDREN'S ROOM
H. COSSITT LIBRARY

The Squeaky, Creaky Bed

By Pat Thomson • Illustrated by Niki Daly

A Doubleday Book for Young Readers

A Doubleday Book for Young Readers
Published by
Random House Children's Books
a division of
Random House, Inc.
1540 Broadway
New York, New York 10036

Doubleday and the anchor with dolphin colophon are registered trademarks of Random House, Inc.

Text copyright © 2003 by Pat Thomson
Illustrations copyright © 2003 by Niki Daly
All rights reserved. No part of this book may be reproduced or transmitted in any form or by
any means, electronic or mechanical, including photocopying, recording, or by any information
storage and retrieval system, without the written permission of the publisher, except where
permitted by law.

Visit us on the Web! www.randomhouse.com/kids
Educators and librarians, for a variety of teaching tools, visit us at
www.randomhouse.com/teachers

Library of Congress Cataloging-in-Publication Data

Thomson, Pat.
  The squeaky, creaky bed / by Pat Thomson ; illustrated by Niki Daly.
      p. cm.
"A Doubleday Book for Young Readers."
Summary: A cumulative tale about a little boy who cannot fall asleep in the noisy old bed at his
grandparents' house.
  ISBN 0-385-74630-X (hardcover)
  ISBN 0-385-90856-3 (lib. bdg.)
[1. Beds—Fiction. 2. Noise—Fiction. 3. Animals—Fiction. 4. Grandparents—Fiction.]
I. Daly, Niki, ill. II. Title.
  PZ7.T3765 Sq 2003
  [E]—dc21
                                                        2002009213

The text of this book is set in 24-point Smile Medium.
Book design by Trish Parcell Watts

Printed in the United States of America
May 2003
10 9 8 7 6 5 4 3 2 1

Once there was a little boy who went
to stay with his grandparents in the country.

He loved
to play in
the woods,

he loved
to paddle
in the stream,
and he loved
his grandparents.

But the house was old,
the furniture was old,
and he did not like the
squeaky, creaky bed.

Every night, Grandmother said good night,
Grandfather said good night,
and the little boy climbed into bed.

Then the bed went

squeak,squeak,creak!

And the little boy cried

WAAUGH! WAAUG

"Don't cry," said Grandmother.
"It's only the squeaky, creaky bed."

"What that boy needs," said Grandfather,
"is a little cat to keep him company."

The next day, he went out to find one.

Just before bedtime,
he brought home a little cat.

Grandmother said good night,
Grandfather said good night,
and the little boy and the cat
climbed into bed.

Then the bed went squeak, squeak, creak!

And the little boy cried

W AAUGH

And the cat mewed

MEEOW! MEEOW!

"Don't cry, little boy.
Don't cry, little cat," said Grandmother.
"It's only the squeaky, creaky bed."

"What that boy needs," said Grandfather,
"is a little dog to keep him company."

The next day, he went out to find one.

Just before bedtime,
he brought home a little dog.

Grandmother said good night,
Grandfather said good night,
and the little boy, the cat, and
the dog climbed into bed.

And the dog barked

Ruff! Ruff!

"Don't cry, little boy.
Don't cry, little cat.
Don't cry, little dog," said Grandmother.
"It's only the squeaky, creaky bed."

"What that boy needs," said Grandfather,
"is a little pig to keep him company."

The next day, he went out to find one.

Just before bedtime,
he brought home a little pig.

Grandmother said good night,
Grandfather said good night,
and the little boy, the cat, the dog,
and the pig climbed into bed.

Then the bed went
squeak, squeak, creak!
And the cat mewed
MEEOW! MEEOW!
And the dog barked
Ruff
And the little boy cried
WAAUGH! WAAUGH!

And the pig snorted

OINK! OINK!

uff!

"Don't cry, little boy.
Don't cry, little cat.
Don't cry, little dog.
Don't cry, little pig," said Grandmother.
"It's only the squeaky, creaky bed."

"What that boy needs," said Grandfather,
"is a parrot to keep him company."

The next day, he went out to find one.

Just before bedtime,
he brought home a parrot.

Grandmother said good night,
Grandfather said good night,
and the little boy, the cat, the dog,
the pig, and the parrot climbed into bed.

Grandfather was so astonished,
he sat down on the bed—
and it BROKE!

"What this boy needs,"
said Grandfather, "is a new bed."

The next day, he went out to find one.

Just before bedtime,
he brought home the new bed.

Grandmother said good night,
Grandfather said good night,
and the little boy, the cat,
the dog, the pig, and the parrot
all climbed into the new bed.

Everything was quiet.
The new bed did not
make a sound.
The little boy held his breath.
And so did the cat,
the dog, the pig,
and the parrot.

UNTIL . . .

The pig snorted
OINK!
OINK!
And the parrot squawked
I know what's wrong!

The parrot flew to the
end of the bed and
perched there. Slowly,
he rocked to and fro, and
quietly, very quietly,
he squawked

squeak, squeak, creak! squeak, sq

creak! squeak, squeak, creak! sque

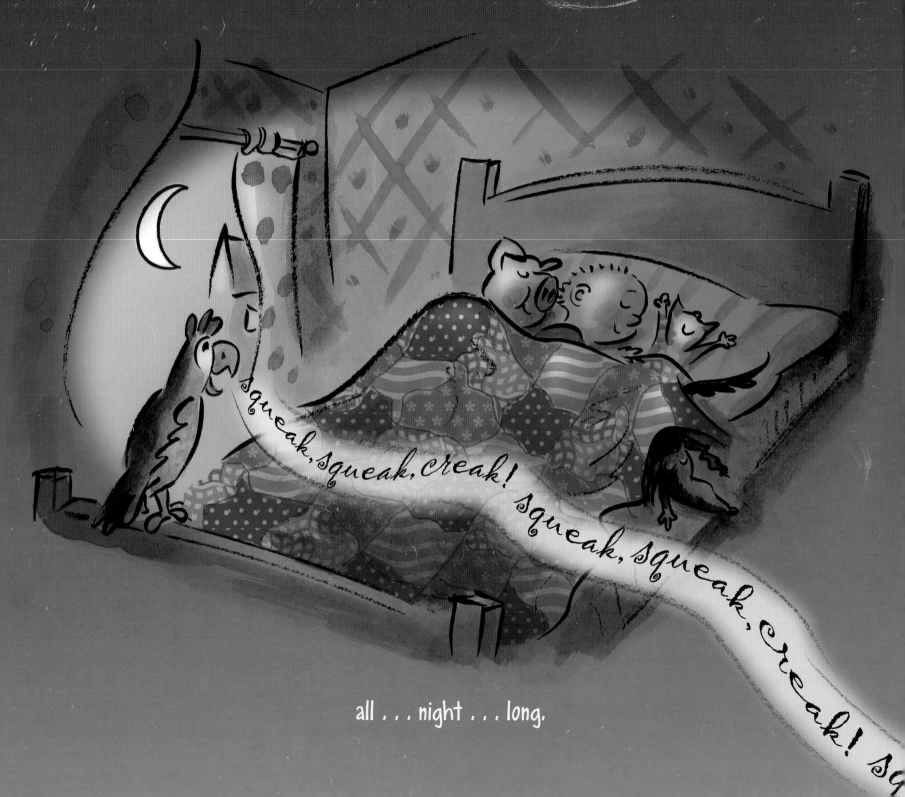